Amy Wild, Animal Talker

The Vanishing Cat

Diana Kimpton

Illustrated by
Desideria Guicciardini

USBORNE

The Clamerkin Clan

Hilton

Amy

Einstein

Plato

Isambard

Willow

Bun

To Aaron

First published in the UK in 2010 by Usborne Publishing Ltd., Usborne House, 83-85 Saffron Hill, London EC1N 8RT, England. www.usborne.com

Text copyright © Diana Kimpton, 2010

Illustrations copyright © Usborne Publishing Ltd., 2010

The right of Diana Kimpton to be identified as the author of this work has been asserted by her in accordance with the Copyright, Designs and Patents Act, 1988.

Cover photograph © Juniors Bildarchiv / Alamy

The name Usborne and the devices ♀ ⊕ are Trade Marks of Usborne Publishing Ltd.

A CIP catalogue record for this book is available from the British Library.

First published in America in 2014 AE.

PB ISBN 9780794529253 ALB ISBN 9781601303202

JFMAMJJASO D/13   02555/2

Printed in Dongguan, Guangdong, China.

CHAPTER ONE

"I'd like to send this, please," said Amy Wild, as she pushed the package across the post office counter.

Miss Pickle, the post lady, glanced at the address. "You're just in time," she said. "The mail for the mainland hasn't left yet."

"Good," barked Hilton, the cairn terrier. He tapped Amy's leg with his paw. "Don't forget the letter."

Amy wasn't surprised to understand what he said. The string of glittering paws she wore around her neck was magic. It gave her the power to talk to animals.

She reached in her pocket and pulled out the letter the dog had mentioned. "There's this too," she said, as she handed it to Miss Pickle. "I've been collecting tokens from the dog food labels to get Hilton a rubber bone."

Miss Pickle peered over the counter and smiled at the terrier. His words had only sounded like barks to her. "Bless him! He's so excited. It's almost as if he understands."

Amy resisted the temptation to tell

her that he did. Her special power had to stay secret – her great-aunt, Granty, had told her so. It was Granty who had given her the necklace when Amy first came to live on Clamerkin Island. And Granty was the only other human in the world who knew that Amy could talk to animals when she was wearing it.

Miss Pickle put a stamp on the letter and tossed it into a sack hanging under a narrow shelf on the back wall. On top of the shelf lay a Siamese cat. She was stretched out full length with two paws and her tail hanging over the edge. She was also fast asleep.

Miss Pickle weighed Amy's package on the scales and stuck on the right number of stamps. Then she tossed that into the sack too.

The package landed with a thud so loud that it woke the cat. Her blue eyes snapped open and she tried to stand up. But the shelf was so narrow that she lost her balance.

"Oh no!" cried Amy, as the cat tumbled over the edge.

Luckily, she didn't fall into the sack. She hit the edge instead and bounced off onto the floor, landing neatly on her feet like cats always do. Then she stuck her nose and tail in the air and rubbed herself against Miss Pickle's legs.

The post lady laughed and tickled the cat's ears. "Silly old Willow. Whenever she falls off that shelf, she always pretends it was what she meant to happen."

"What's she fallen off?" asked Hilton, who was too small to have seen what had happened.

Willow jumped onto the counter and looked down at the terrier. "I didn't fall," she insisted. "I just sort of slid, deliberately on purpose."

"Oh dear," said Miss Pickle, who could only hear barking and mewing. "I do hope Willow and Hilton aren't going to fight."

"I'm sure they won't," said Amy. She knew the cat and dog were good friends. As if to prove her right, Willow jumped down on Amy's side of the counter and sniffed noses with Hilton. Then she strode out of the post office.

Amy watched her go. Then she handed Miss Pickle the money for the postage, said goodbye and started to leave.

"Wait a minute!" called the post lady, waving a teddy bear at Amy. "This belongs to Benny Croft. He must have dropped it when his mom was telling me about the work they're having done to Holly Cottage. I can't leave the post office unattended, so I wonder if you could take it back for me?"

"Of course I can," said Amy. She tucked the bear in the crook of her arm and set off with Hilton by her side.

Willow was sitting outside in the sunshine, washing her face with her paws. Amy bent down so she was close enough to speak to the cat without anyone else noticing. "Are you all right?" she asked. "I hope you didn't hurt yourself when you fell."

Willow turned her head away to show she was offended. "I've told you before. I didn't fall. I got down quite deliberately." Then she shook herself from head to tail and changed the subject. "Have you heard about the clan meeting?"

Amy nodded. "Einstein told me during history." He was the school cat and, like Hilton, Willow and Amy, he belonged to the clan – the group of animals that looked after Clamerkin Island.

"Einstein told me too," said Hilton. "He said there's a problem we need to solve."

"I wonder what it is," purred Willow. "I love solving problems."

"So do I," said Amy. She was eager to learn more about this new one, but the meeting wasn't due to start for ages. And in the meantime, she had an errand to run.

"Come on," she called to Hilton. "We've got a bear to return to its owner."

CHAPTER TWO

Amy and Hilton walked together up the cobbled street and turned into the narrow lane that led to Holly Cottage. Normally it was very quiet here – just the sound of the wind in the trees and the birds singing. But today the air was full of noise. There was banging and sawing and a deep, rumbling sound.

Amy saw the source of the rumbling

as soon as she reached the gate. She wasn't the only one looking. A tabby cat sat by the fence, staring adoringly at the bright orange machine.

"Wonderful things – cement mixers," he purred.

"Hello, Isambard," said Amy, as she stroked his head. "Are you keeping an eye on the builders?"

"They're doing a wonderful job on the extension," said the cat, nodding his head toward the newest part of the building. "I wonder what they're going to do next."

Their conversation was brought to a sudden stop when Cathy Croft opened the front door and stepped outside. She was carrying baby Benny in one arm and waving at Amy with the other. "Have you come to visit us?" she asked, as she picked her way between the piles of sand and rubble that littered the front yard. "If so, you're just in time. We're leaving to stay with my mom for a few days to escape all this mess."

"Miss Pickle asked me to bring you this," said Amy, holding out the bear. "You left it in the post office."

Benny squealed with delight and grabbed his toy. Then he wrapped both arms around it and pulled it close to his chest.

Cathy laughed. "He's determined not to lose that again. Thanks for bringing it back."

Isambard rubbed against Amy's

legs to attract her attention. "Find out what's happening," he mewed.

Amy took the hint. She smiled and asked, "How's the work coming along?"

"It's almost finished," said Cathy. "The builders are just putting the finishing touches on the extension. Then they're going to build a patio and fill in our slimy, old pond."

"That's a shame," said Amy. "I like ponds."

"So do I," said Cathy. "But they're not safe for toddlers. If we left that one there, I'd worry all the time that Benny might fall in."

She turned to go back to the house. Then she paused and looked at Amy.

"Can you stay for a while and play with Benny? He loves seeing you, and I could pack so much quicker if I didn't have to entertain him as well."

Amy agreed willingly. She always enjoyed visiting Holly Cottage, and she knew Mom and Dad wouldn't mind, provided she called them from Cathy's phone to let them know where she was. So playing with the baby was the perfect way to fill the time until the meeting.

She and Hilton followed Cathy inside and settled down on the carpet with Benny and his toys. "Is this supposed to be fun?" asked the dog, as the baby hit him on the head with a stuffed giraffe.

"We're not here to enjoy ourselves," said Amy. She took the giraffe away and started to build a tower of blocks to distract the baby's attention. "We're here to keep an eye on Benny so Cathy can do her packing."

Hilton cheered up. "I like helping people." He looked thoughtful as he moved his tail out of Benny's reach. "I wonder what this new problem for the clan is."

Amy was curious about it too. But she knew one thing for certain. The problem was sure to involve an animal. Only the animals on Clamerkin Island knew they could turn to the clan for help. The humans didn't even know it existed.

An hour later, it was time for Benny's dinner and almost time for the meeting. So Amy said goodbye and set off for home with Hilton. "Enjoy your break from the builders," she called, as she stepped out of Holly Cottage.

"I'm sure we will," said Cathy. "And thanks again for all your help. I couldn't have managed without you."

Amy and Hilton walked along the road and down the cobbled street to the Primrose Tea Room, where they lived. Mom and Dad were busy serving customers while Granty was in the kitchen, baking cakes for the next day.

She smiled when Amy walked into the room. "Did you manage to mail everything?"

Amy nodded. "Miss Pickle said I was just in time. The mail to the mainland hadn't left." Then she pulled all the money from her pocket and handed it to Granty. "It wasn't as much as you thought. Here's the change."

Hilton ran into the hall and scratched impatiently at the back door. "Come on," he barked. "It's time for the meeting."

His words brought Plato, the parrot, flying from his perch in the living room. He was a clan member, too, so he flew beside Amy and Hilton as they ran down the garden and dived into the clump of bushes at the far end.

Amy pushed her way through the branches until she reached the clearing in the middle. This was the clan's almost-secret meeting place. Einstein, the white Persian cat from the school, was already there. So was the fat, black cat who lived at the bakery.

"Hello, Bun," said Amy, as she sat down beside him. Then she glanced around the clearing and noticed there was no sign of Willow. That was unusual – the Siamese cat was usually the first to arrive.

At that moment, Isambard ran into the clearing. "Sorry I'm late," he puffed. "My human was resetting some spark plugs, and I couldn't resist watching."

"Don't worry," squawked Plato. "You're not last. We're still waiting for Willow."

The tabby cat looked surprised. "That's not like her. She's never late."

"She is today," said Hilton.

"Maybe she stopped off for something to eat," Bun suggested.

Isambard shook his head. "*You* might do that, but she wouldn't. She likes to be early for meetings."

"And she definitely knows about this one," said Amy, as a pang of anxiety stirred deep in her stomach. "She told us so this afternoon."

Amy had just finished speaking when there was a rustling in the bushes. She looked toward the sound, hoping to see Willow emerge from among the leaves.

But she didn't. The new arrival was a large, brown duck. She waddled onto the grass and bobbed her head up and down in greeting. "I hope I'm in the right place. Are you the clan?"

"We're most of it," squawked Plato.

"We're just waiting for the last cat to get here."

"Perhaps we should start without her," said Einstein. He walked over and stood beside the duck. "This is Petunia. She asked me to call the meeting, and it doesn't seem fair to keep her waiting."

The rest of the clan murmured their agreement. "We can tell Willow all about it when she finally turns up," barked Hilton.

Amy thought that sounded reasonable. But her worry about the missing cat was stronger now. She had never been to a clan meeting without Willow before. It felt very strange not having her there.

CHAPTER THREE

Einstein pushed Petunia forward with his paw. "Tell everyone about your problem."

The duck waggled her tail from side to side and started to speak. "It's not *my* problem. It's my two friends – Harvey and Sid."

"Are they ducks, too?" asked Hilton.

"No. They're frogs, and they're best friends. They've lived together in the

same pond ever since they were
tadpoles. But now it's going to be filled
in, so they're going to be homeless."

"Save the pond!" squawked Plato.
"We'll start a protest. I've seen lots on TV.
People lie down in front of bulldozers."

Bun's eyes opened wide in horror.

"I'm not doing that. It's much too dangerous. Just thinking about it makes me hungry."

"Thinking about anything makes *you* hungry," said Isambard. Then he looked at Plato and added, "I'm not big on the bulldozer thing either. Do protesters do anything else?"

"Oh yes!" squawked the parrot, hopping from one foot to the other with excitement. "They shout and wave signs and stuff like that."

"Cats and dogs can't wave signs," said Hilton.

"But Amy could," said Plato. "And we could keep her company."

The clan looked expectantly at Amy. But before she had time to say anything, Petunia gave a loud quack. "Stop! You've got it all wrong. We don't want you to save the pond. We think it's right to get rid of it."

There was a moment of confused silence. Then Amy had a flash of inspiration. "Are you talking about the pond at Holly Cottage? The one they're filling in to keep the baby safe."

"That's right," quacked Petunia. "I don't blame Benny's parents for doing that. I'd want to keep my babies away from water, too, if they didn't know how to swim."

Bun brightened up. "Does that mean I don't have to stop any bulldozers?"

"I suppose it does," said Plato, his shoulders slumped in disappointment.

Hilton stared at the duck. "I'm confused. What do you actually want us to do?"

"Help Harvey and Sid to move," said Petunia, with another waggle of her tail. "They're too big for me to carry, and I'm worried they'll get hurt if they try to hop to another pond by themselves. They've never been out of that garden before, so they have no idea how to avoid danger."

"That's easy to fix," said Amy. "I can carry them to their new pond if you tell me where it is."

Petunia looked slightly embarrassed. "That's the other part of the problem. I can't find one that's suitable. All the ponds I've looked at are full of frogs already, and Harvey and Sid would prefer to live on their own."

Plato perked up again. "A pond hunt! That's almost as good as a 'save the pond' protest."

"It's a shame Willow isn't here," said Bun. "She hears lots of gossip in the post office. She's sure to know about the local ponds."

"I wish she'd turn up," said Isambard. "It doesn't feel right without her."

His words made Amy's stomach knot with anxiety. Willow should be here by now. Suppose something was wrong. Suppose the Siamese cat was in trouble and needed the clan's help?

That idea spurred Amy into action. She jumped to her feet and urged the others to do the same. "Come on!" she said. "We've got to find out if Willow's all right."

As the rest of the clan barked, mewed and squawked their agreement, Amy remembered Petunia. She crouched down beside the duck and said, "I'm sorry – we can't stay any longer. We've got to reach the post office before it closes."

"Good luck!" quacked the duck, as she waddled out of the way. "But what should I tell Harvey and Sid?"

"Tell them we'll come for them on Saturday morning," Amy promised. "We're sure to have found a pond by then." Then she pushed her way through the bushes and sprinted up the garden. The rest of the clan raced with her, except for Plato, who flew instead.

They ran along the path beside the Primrose. Then they dashed into the street and headed for the post office. Its front door was open, but there was no sign of Willow.

"Maybe she's behind the counter," suggested Hilton.

"Someone needs to go inside and check," said Einstein. He stared at Amy and added, "Someone tall enough to see over the top."

Bun stared at her too. "Go and buy something."

"I can't," said Amy. "I don't have any money." Then she remembered her trip to Holly Cottage, and that gave her the excuse she needed.

She stepped through the door with Hilton by her side and Plato on her shoulder. Then she walked up to the counter and smiled at Miss Pickle. "Benny was happy to get his bear back," she said.

"That's good," replied the post lady. But she wasn't looking at Amy. She was too busy staring at the three cats peering around the door frame. She took off her glasses, polished them on her sleeve and balanced them back on her nose. Then she stared at the cats again and gave a disappointed sigh.

"Is something wrong?" asked Amy.

Miss Pickle sighed again. "I'd hoped one of those cats was my Willow." She pointed at some sardines on a plate on the floor. "She always has a little snack when I have my lunch. But she didn't come for it today, and that's not like her at all."

"So it's not just our meeting she's missed," squawked Plato.

"There really *is* something wrong," whined Hilton.

Amy thought so too. Then she suddenly remembered something. "Willow fell off the shelf earlier," she said to the post lady. "Do you think she might have hurt herself?"

"I'm sure she didn't," said Miss Pickle. "She's tumbled off that shelf lots of times without coming to any harm." She chuckled and added, "One of these days my silly old cat will land in the sack with all the mail."

Amy glanced at the shelf. "But the sack isn't there!"

"That's because Fred's taken it down to the ferry," said Miss Pickle. Then she gasped and put her hand to her mouth. "Oh no! What if Willow has fallen inside? She won't be able to get out until it's opened again. And, by then, she'll be on the mainland."

"She'll never find her way home from there," cried Amy. A shiver of fear ran down her back. She couldn't bear the thought of never seeing the Siamese cat again.

CHAPTER FOUR

Plato flapped his wings in alarm. "We've got to do something," he squawked.

"Like what?" asked Hilton.

Amy glanced at the clock on the wall. "Has the ferry left yet?" she asked.

"Not for another five minutes," said Miss Pickle. There was a hint of hope in her voice as she added, "Maybe there's time to rescue Willow before it sails." Then her shoulders slumped as she sighed, "But I can't leave the post office unattended – it's against the rules."

"The rules can't stop me," said Amy. She spun around and raced out of the post office. Hilton ran with her and Plato flew overhead.

Isambard, Einstein and Bun didn't have to ask what was happening. They'd heard enough of the conversation to know that Willow's safety was at stake. So they hurtled down the cobbled street with Amy, running as fast as their legs would carry them.

Amy raced on and on, ignoring the curious eyes of passers-by. She didn't care what they thought. All that mattered was saving Willow.

She reached the bottom of the hill and skidded around the corner to the harbor. To her relief, the ferry was still there. But its engine was already

running, and the sailors were undoing the ropes that tied it to the shore.

"Wait!" shrieked Amy.

"Don't go!" shouted Hilton and Plato.

"You've got Willow!" yelled Einstein and Isambard.

Only Bun stayed quiet. He was too out of breath to say anything.

They made so much noise that the sailors looked in their direction. To them, the animals were just barking and mewing and squawking. But they could understand Amy.

"Don't go," she yelled. "You've got the post office cat in the mailbag."

To her relief, they called to the captain to stop the ferry. Then they retied the ropes and put back the gangway.

The captain walked down it with the mail sack over his shoulder. "Are you sure there's a cat in here?" he asked, as he put it down in front of Amy.

"As sure as I can be," she replied. "Willow's definitely disappeared, and Miss Pickle says she's always falling off the shelf above the sack. So that *must* be where she is."

"It certainly sounds like it," said the captain. "We'd better let her out." He gently laid the sack on its side and started to untie the rope that held it closed.

While Amy watched him, she wondered how Willow would behave when she was rescued. Would she run out, delighted to be free? Or would she creep out, feeling slightly foolish. Most probably she would do exactly the same as she had when she fell off the shelf – she'd walk out with her tail in the air, pretending she had gotten into the sack on purpose.

As the captain undid the last knot, Amy pulled the sack wide open to let the Siamese cat escape. But all her ideas were wrong. Willow didn't run out or creep out or walk out. She didn't appear at all.

"I can't see a cat," said the captain.

"Maybe she's trapped at the bottom," said Amy.

The captain picked up the sack and slowly poured its contents onto the ground. By the time it was empty, there was a pile of letters and packages on the dock. But there was still no sign of Willow.

The captain gave the sack a last

shake to prove there was nothing left inside. "I'm sorry, young lady. Wherever that cat is, it's definitely not here."

Amy felt a wave of disappointment surge through her. It was tinged with embarrassment. "I'm sorry I've wasted your time," she said to the captain. "I hope you're not upset."

"Of course I'm not," he replied, with a broad smile. "You made a good guess. It's not your fault it was wrong."

Amy helped him put all the mail back into the sack and watched him carry it back onto the ferry. Then she turned and walked sadly back to the post office with the rest of the clan. There was no need to run anymore.

"Don't feel bad," said Hilton. "Miss Pickle was as sure as us that Willow was in that sack."

"And she'll be as disappointed as we are when she hears we haven't found her," said Plato.

"Not if Willow's come back while

we were away," said Einstein. "Maybe she'll be waiting for us when we get there."

His suggestion filled Amy with hope. But as soon as she stepped into the post office, she knew he was wrong. Miss Pickle was waiting anxiously behind the counter, and the Siamese cat wasn't with her.

"I'm sorry," said Amy. "We got there in time, but Willow wasn't in the sack."

"I suppose I should be pleased," sighed Miss Pickle. "At least she wasn't trapped in there in the dark. But she still hasn't come home. And she still hasn't had anything to eat. I'm sure something's happened to her."

*

No one in the clan knew what to do next. So they went back to the almost-secret meeting place to think. It was deserted. Petunia had gone home.

"I don't like it here without Willow," wailed Bun, staring at the patch of grass where the Siamese cat usually sat.

"Neither do I," said Hilton. He looked as miserable as everyone else. His steps had lost their bounce, and his tail hung low.

"Maybe she's been catnapped," Einstein suggested. "The children read a story about catnappers yesterday."

Isambard gave a snort of disapproval. "Don't believe everything you hear. Stories aren't real."

Bun's mouth dropped open in astonishment. "That's weird. You sound just like Willow."

"You're right," said Amy. "Willow would say that if she was here." She thought for a moment. Then she added, "But I think she'd also ask how we're going to find a pond."

"The pond hunt!" shrieked Plato. "I've been so worried about Willow that I'd forgotten all about it."

"We can't do that," said Amy. "We've got to help Harvey and Sid. Even with one member missing, we're still the clan."

CHAPTER FIVE

Amy left home extra early the next morning. She wanted to check on Willow on her way to school. The post office wasn't open yet, but Miss Pickle opened the door when she saw Amy coming.

Amy guessed immediately that the news was bad. The post lady looked so tired and sad. Her face was red and blotchy from crying.

"Willow still hasn't come home." She sighed. "She's missed supper and breakfast now as well as yesterday's snack. I couldn't sleep without her curled up beside me on my bed. So I got up early and made these posters on my computer." She took a sheet of paper from a pile on the counter and handed it to Amy.

Printed across the top in big, bold letters was the word LOST. And below the word was a photo of a very familiar Siamese cat. Amy's eyes pricked with tears as she read the poster. "I can help you put these up," she said. "The more people who see them, the more likely she is to be found."

LOST

IF FOUND,
PLEASE CONTACT MISS PICKLE AT
CLAMERKIN POST OFFICE

"I hope so," said Miss Pickle, with a weak smile. "But it feels as if my cat's vanished into thin air."

Amy looked unsuccessfully for Willow on the way to school. But she did manage to put up several posters on the fences and trees. She pinned one to the school gate. Then she walked around the playground, handing out posters to all the other children and asking if they had spotted the Siamese cat. But no one had seen her anywhere. Miss Pickle was right – Willow seemed to have vanished.

When the bell rang, Amy lined up with the rest of her class and walked into the classroom. She gave a poster to her teacher, Mrs. Damson. Then she sat down at her desk and tried to push her worries about Willow out of her mind. There was nothing more she could do to find the cat at the moment, and she needed to concentrate on her lessons.

The first one was math. Amy gazed around the room while Mrs. Damson handed out the worksheets. A large map of Clamerkin Island hung on one wall, and the sight of it gave her an idea. Although she couldn't help Willow while she was at school, there might be something she could do to help Harvey and Sid.

But the map was too far away for her to read from her desk. She needed to get much closer to find the information she needed. Luckily, the electric pencil sharpener stood on a shelf beside the map. All she needed now was an excuse to use it.

She waited until everyone was busy working. Then she pressed hard on her pencil until the lead snapped, stood up and walked over to the sharpener.

Einstein was sitting near it. He nodded his head toward the map. "Can you find a pond on there?" he mewed. "I've already tried but I don't understand the different colors."

Amy made sure that everyone was too busy to notice her talking to the cat. Then she whispered back, so quietly that only he could hear. "We're looking for tiny patches of blue – that's the color of water."

She stared intently at the map, searching for as many ponds as she could find. She was concentrating so hard that she didn't hear her teacher walk up behind her.

"What's so interesting?" asked Mrs. Damson.

The sound of her voice made Amy jump. "I was just looking," she said.

"I could see that," said her teacher. "But what were you looking for?"

Amy's mind raced as she wondered what to say. She couldn't explain about Harvey and Sid without risking the secret of the necklace. But a half-truth might work. "Ponds!" she said. "I was looking for ponds that might have frogs for me to watch."

Mrs. Damson laughed. "You'll only find really big ones on that map. The little ponds that frogs like are too small to show up."

Amy sighed and pushed her pencil into the sharpener. The map had seemed like the perfect solution to her problem. But it obviously wasn't.

Einstein nudged her hand with his nose. "What are we going to do?" he mewed.

Amy wanted to answer him. But she couldn't. Her teacher was still too close. She was busy examining a shelf of books, but she'd be sure to notice Amy talking to the cat.

Mrs. Damson tapped Amy on the shoulder. "If you don't stop sharpening that pencil soon, there won't be any left to write with." Then she held out a book. "Frogs don't just live in ponds. Take a look in here and you'll learn all about them."

Amy didn't get a chance to look at the book at break – she was too busy talking to her friends. The whole class had overheard her conversation with Mrs. Damson, and everyone who had a pond at home was inviting her to visit it. But all their ponds already had frogs in them, so they weren't any good for Harvey and Sid.

To her relief, the excitement had died down by lunchtime, so she managed to get away from everyone else. She crept into a far corner of the playground, put one of Willow's posters on the wall and sat down to look at the book. Einstein insisted on peering at the pages at the same time, although he couldn't read.

"I can look at the pictures," he grumbled, as she gently moved him

out of the way. "Look there's a frog –
and another frog – and another frog."

"Of course there is," sighed Amy,
"that's what the book's about." She
flipped quickly through the pages

until she found the section she needed. "Frogs like damp places," she read aloud. "They like to live near ponds and streams." Then she stopped and grinned at Einstein.

"Why have you stopped?" he asked.

"Because we've found the answer," said Amy, as she snapped the book shut. "We don't have to find a pond for Harvey and Sid. We can find a stream for them instead."

Amy didn't see Einstein for the rest of the afternoon. It was story time for the younger children, and he could never resist listening to that. But he met her outside the gate when school finished.

"I need to talk to you," he said in a serious voice. "I've discovered something important about frogs."

"You'll have to tell me later," said Amy. She didn't want to think about Harvey and Sid at the moment. She was too busy handing out posters of Willow to all the parents who were picking up their children from preschool.

It was difficult trying to solve two problems at once. The frogs were important, but so was Willow. Amy hoped desperately that she would never have to choose between them.

CHAPTER SIX

By the time the clan gathered in their almost-secret meeting place, Willow's picture was all over town. And everyone knew that the Siamese cat was officially lost.

"We've got a poster in our shop window," said Bun.

"So do we," said Amy. "And Granty's let me put them on all the tables in the tea room."

"Great," said Isambard. "The more people who see them the better."

The others nodded their agreement. Then Plato flapped his wings to attract their attention. "Don't forget Harvey and Sid. We promised to move them on Saturday morning. So we've only got until tomorrow to find a pond."

Einstein stood up, fluffed out his coat and stuck his tail in the air. "I've discovered something very important about frogs," he announced.

"So have I," Amy interrupted. "They like living near streams so we don't need to find a pond at all."

Einstein whisked his tail crossly. "That's not what I was going to say," he muttered. But no one was listening. The others were too excited about Amy's good news.

"There's a nice stream beside Desdemona's field," said Isambard.

"Would that be safe?" asked Bun. "She's a very big cow with very big feet."

"She could easily squash a frog," Plato agreed.

Amy nodded her agreement. "But the stream's long. There's sure to be a part where Harvey and Sid could live without being stepped on."

"Let's go and look," barked Hilton. He jumped to his feet, eager to leave.

But Einstein stepped in front of him to bar his way. "What about Willow?"

he asked. "Shouldn't we be looking for her?"

Amy felt torn in two. It felt wrong to stop searching for the Siamese cat while they helped the frogs. But it felt equally wrong to ignore Harvey and Sid.

"Willow won't be by the stream," said Isambard. "I'm sure of that. Streams are wet, and cats don't like wet."

His comment gave Amy an idea. "Let's split up," she suggested. "I'll go with Hilton and Plato to find a good place for frogs, while you three cats search for Willow in the places you know cats like. That way we can help everyone at once."

The clan arranged to meet at Holly Cottage the next morning to pick up the frogs. Then they slipped through the gap between the hedge and the shed and set off in different directions. The cats ran off to check Willow's favorite places, while Amy, Hilton and Plato headed toward the stream.

Amy was halfway there when she remembered Einstein had wanted to tell them something important – something about frogs. But it was too late to ask him about it now. She'd have to wait until tomorrow. She hoped it wasn't so important that they would have to change their plans.

When Amy, Hilton and Plato reached the stream by Desdemona's field, the cow ambled over to meet them. Cleo, the goat, trotted by her side.

"Have you seen Willow?" asked Amy.

"Not since she went missing," mooed Desdemona.

"We're very worried about her," bleated Cleo.

Amy was surprised they had already heard the bad news. "How do you know she's lost?" she asked. She was sure there weren't any posters near the field.

"Barney, the border collie, found out when he went to the Primrose with his human," Desdemona explained.

"And he told all the birds who live near his cottage," said Cleo.

"Are you sure?" asked the cow. "I thought he only told the pigeons and the magpie."

"Maybe I exaggerated a little," said Cleo, looking slightly embarrassed. "But he definitely told *some* birds and they told others, and now every animal on Clamerkin Island is trying to find

Willow." She glanced at Desdemona, as if she expected to be corrected again. Then she added, "Well, almost every animal anyway."

Amy was delighted to hear that. So was Hilton. He jumped up and down, wagging his tail in excitement. "That's brilliant," he barked. "With so many of us looking, we're sure to find her soon."

"She's not in this field," said Desdemona. "Cleo and I have searched it very carefully."

"So you don't have to," added the goat. "I suppose that means you'll go now."

Amy shook her head. "Willow's not our only problem at the moment. We're

trying to help some frogs as well."
Then she told them all about Harvey
and Sid and how they needed a new
place to live. But she didn't mention
the cow's big feet because she didn't
want to hurt her feelings.

Cleo was less sensitive. "Don't put
the frogs in our part of the stream,"
she said, as she butted her head gently
against Desdemona. "She'll squash
them if she steps on them."

The cow nodded sadly. "Cleo's right.
I'd try to be careful. But frogs are
green and so is grass. I might have
trouble telling the difference."

"It doesn't matter anyway," said
Amy, as she glanced at the stream.
The water tumbled and swirled as it

ran swiftly downhill. "Harvey and Sid are used to a pond. I think they'd prefer a spot where the water doesn't move as fast."

Plato soared into the air and followed the path of the stream across the next field. Then he flew back and reported, "The ground's flat in the far corner, so the water moves more slowly. I think it would be perfect for frogs."

Amy wasn't quite so sure. Neither was Hilton. "Are there anymore cows with big feet?" he asked.

"No," squawked Plato, as he landed on the fence. "The field's completely empty."

"But it isn't always," said Cleo.

"Mistletoe, the donkey, lives in there sometimes."

"And his feet would squash frogs just as easily as mine," added Desdemona.

Amy sighed. Finding the right place for Harvey and Sid wasn't as easy as she'd hoped. Then she noticed an area of long grass and bushes that was fenced off from both fields. The stream ran in on one side and out the other, but she couldn't see what it did in the middle.

"What's that?" she asked Cleo and Desdemona.

"It's just a patch of ground the farmer doesn't use," the goat replied. "It's too boggy and wet for grazing or for growing crops."

"But it might be right for frogs," said Amy, as she climbed over the fence. Hilton wiggled underneath to join her, but Plato stayed behind.

"I'll leave the decision to you," he squawked. "My wings need a rest."

Amy pushed her way through the branches, following the path of the stream across the flat, muddy ground. The water wasn't rushing here. It trickled so slowly that the stream had widened into a shallow pool.

"It looks a little like a pond," said Hilton. He put his nose to the ground and sniffed along the edges of the water. "I can't smell any other frogs. Harvey and Sid would have this place all to themselves."

"It's perfect," said Amy. "All we've got to do now is move them here tomorrow morning."

But her excitement about finding the right spot was dampened by her anxiety about Willow. The frogs' problem was sorted out – well, almost anyway. But they still hadn't solved the mystery of the vanishing cat.

CHAPTER SEVEN

Amy hoped they would find good news waiting for them when they got back to the Primrose. But there was just Isambard slumped unhappily on the doorstep.

"We searched everywhere we could think of," he mewed. "All the cozy spots she likes to have a nap and the places where she sits to watch what's going on. But there was no sign of her anywhere. Not even a stray hair."

Amy found it hard to sleep that night. She was too worried about Willow. So the next morning, she didn't go straight to Holly Cottage with Hilton and Plato. Instead, they stopped in at the post office to see if the Siamese cat had returned.

They immediately knew that she hadn't. Willow's favorite shelf was still empty, and Miss Pickle was sobbing gently behind the counter.

"I don't think I'm ever going to see her again," she cried, as she dabbed her eyes with a tissue.

Amy shuddered. Suppose Miss Pickle

was right. Suppose the Siamese cat was gone forever. That was such a dreadful idea that she couldn't bear to think about it.

Neither could Hilton. "I wish she hadn't said that," he whimpered, as they left the post office.

"So do I," said Plato quietly.

As they approached Holly Cottage, they decided not to mention Miss Pickle's fears to the rest of the clan. The three cats waiting outside already looked miserable enough. There was no need to make them feel even worse.

The sight of the white Persian cat made Amy remember his news. "What was it you wanted to tell us yesterday?" she asked. "You said it was something important about frogs."

Einstein jumped to his feet and purred happily, obviously enjoying being the center of attention. Then he announced, "If you kiss a frog, he turns into a prince."

"What's a prince?" asked Bun. "Can you eat it?"

The others ignored him. They were all too busy trying not to giggle. Only Hilton failed — he rolled on the ground, howling with laughter.

Isambard stepped forward and stood nose to nose with the white cat. "How many times do I have to tell you? Stories aren't real. You must stop believing everything you hear."

"But it sounded so true," said Einstein. He stared at Amy with big, pleading eyes. "Do you think it might be?"

Amy forced herself not to smile while she shook her head. "Isambard's right. It is just a story. I've heard it before."

She watched sadly as the white cat's tail drooped with disappointment. Maybe the best thing to do was to change the subject.

"Let's go and move Harvey and Sid," she said, as she stepped through the gate and led the way to the tiny pond. Benny and his parents were still away and the builders didn't work on Saturdays, so there were no humans around to see what they were doing.

At first, it looked as if there were no frogs either. Then a green face poked out from under a rock. "Are you the clan?" he asked.

Amy nodded. "Did Petunia tell you we were coming?"

"Yes," said the frog, as he hopped

into the open. "But she is a duck, and ducks often get things wrong." He turned and shouted to someone behind him. "It's all right, Sid. It really is them."

A slightly smaller frog peered nervously from under the same rock. "Are you sure it's safe to come out?"

"I'm positive," said Harvey. Then he turned to Amy and added quietly, "I'm sorry about Sid. He's a bundle of nerves at the moment, what with all the noise and everything."

Amy smiled sympathetically as she remembered the noise the builders were making when she took back Benny's bear. "I'm sure you'll like your new home. It's nice and quiet."

"And very damp," added Hilton.

"It sounds perfect," said Harvey.

Sid said nothing. He just looked scared.

Amy reached into her pocket and pulled out a small cloth bag she had brought with her. Then she bent down beside the frogs. "Jump in here and I'll carry you to the stream."

Harvey did as he was told, but Sid backed away. "Stream!" he shrieked. "I thought we were going to another pond."

"It's almost a pond," said Hilton. "It's very shallow and the water's only moving a tiny bit."

Amy slid the bag closer to Sid. "Hop in!"

This time the nervous frog did as he was told. He jumped over the edge and hopped as close to Harvey as he could get.

Einstein sidled over to Amy and rubbed his head against her hand. "Try just one kiss," he pleaded. "Just to see if it works."

"No!" said Amy.

"Please," begged Einstein. "It can't do any harm."

Amy peeked at the two frogs snuggled together in the bag. Their skin looked green,  damp and uninviting. She had no desire to kiss either of them, and she was sure she would terrify Sid if she tried. "Let's get one thing clear," she whispered so quietly that only the white cat could hear. "I will never, *ever* kiss a frog."

"Okay," sighed Einstein. "But it was worth asking." Then he brightened up and purred, "What should we do instead?"

"Let's get going!" said Amy, as she picked up the bag with Harvey and Sid safely inside. Then she set off for the stream with Hilton and Plato. The three cats came too, following a little way behind.

The spot they had found for the frogs was further away than Amy remembered. But it was still just as perfect. The slow-moving stream looked calm and peaceful in the morning sunshine. A gentle breeze rustled the reeds, and dragonflies hovered low over the water.

"Here we are," said Amy, as she put down the bag. "Welcome to your new home."

Harvey jumped out right away and

looked around. "It's wonderful," he croaked. "It's much better than our old pond."

Sid was more cautious. He peeked nervously over the edge of the bag and asked, "Are you sure it's safe?"

"I'm positive," said Amy.

"There aren't any cows," added Plato. "Or donkeys, or any other animals that might step on you."

Sid stared at them with big, round eyes. "That's not what I'm worried about. It's strange noises in the night that scare me."

Amy felt puzzled. The builders didn't work at night. So what noises was Sid talking about?

CHAPTER EIGHT

Amy smiled at Sid. "I'm sure you won't hear any strange noises here. There might be an owl, but you're used to those."

To her surprise, Sid smiled back. "In that case, I'm going to like it here," he said. He hopped out of the bag, looking more cheerful than she had ever seen him. Then he settled down beside Harvey and added, "I stopped liking our old pond as soon as that spooky voice started calling."

"When was that?" asked Hilton.

"Two days ago," Sid replied.

Isambard pricked up his ears. "That's a coincidence! Willow went missing two days ago."

Amy looked at him and then at the frogs. Was Isambard right about it being a coincidence? Or could the two things be connected? "Tell us more about this spooky voice. Can you understand what it's saying?"

"No," said Sid. "It's all muffled. We can't make out individual words."

"Haven't the builders noticed it?" asked Hilton.

Harvey shook his head. "They make such a racket that they don't hear it, and neither do we when they're working. But we can hear it when they're not there."

"*We* didn't hear it when we were there this morning," said Einstein.

"Neither did we," said Sid. "It got quieter and quieter during the night and then it stopped completely."

Amy's suspicions were stronger now. "I think that voice might be Willow's. What if she's stuck somewhere in the new extension and can't get out."

Bun gasped with horror. "She won't have had anything to eat or drink for two whole days."

"That would explain why the noise has stopped," whined Hilton. "She'll be too weak to call for help anymore."

Amy's mouth went dry with fear. "Come on," she yelled. "We've got to get her out before it's too late." Then she started to run back the way they had come. Hilton and the cats galloped beside her, racing toward the town. Plato flew above them, flapping his wings as hard as he could.

Amy had never run so fast for so long. Soon her legs were aching, and she was gasping for breath. Her whole body wanted to stop, but she forced herself to keep going. Willow was in danger. They had to save her.

As they raced down the main street, Amy remembered their other mad rush to rescue the Siamese cat when they thought she was trapped in the mailbag. Was that really only two days ago? It felt much longer.

The cats stopped at the door of the post office. But Plato and Hilton went inside with Amy. Miss Pickle looked up in surprise. So did the customer she was serving. Amy was pleased to see that it was Granty.

"Whatever's the matter?" asked Miss Pickle. "You look very hot and flustered."

"It's Willow," gasped Amy, as she struggled to get her breath back. "I think she's stuck in the new extension at Holly Cottage."

"I must save her," cried Miss Pickle. She lifted the flap in the counter and stepped through the gap to Amy's side. Then she stopped. "But I can't leave the post office unattended."

"I'll look after it," said Granty. "You go with Amy, and I'll call the builders to ask them to meet you there."

Amy was surprised how fast Miss Pickle could run. When they reached Holly Cottage, they found it was deserted. The builders hadn't arrived yet.

"Willow! Willow!" called Miss Pickle, as she picked her way across the messy yard to the extension. The cats called, too, and so did Amy. But Hilton stayed quiet. He put his nose to the ground and started to sniff along the new wall.

Amy climbed onto a pile of wood and peered through the window. The room was completely bare. She couldn't see Willow, and she couldn't see anywhere

the cat might be stuck. But the noise
Sid had heard must have come from
somewhere.

Suddenly Hilton barked. Amy saw he
had his face close to a special brick that
was full of holes. She jumped off the
wood and bent down beside him.

"That's an airbrick," said Miss Pickle. "It leads into the space under the floorboards."

"Willow! Willow!" Amy called through the holes. Then she put her ear against the airbrick and listened carefully. At first, there was silence. Then she heard the most welcome sound in the whole world. It was very quiet, but it was definitely the mew of a Siamese cat.

At exactly that moment, one of the builders arrived. So did the vet – Granty must have been busy on the phone. "Willow's in there," Amy shouted, as she pointed at the airbrick. "I can hear her."

"She must have gotten under the

floor when we had the boards up to do the wiring," said the builder. "It never occurred to me to check for cats before we put them back down."

He led everyone inside and pried up one of the floorboards again. Then he looked into the gap and shook his head. "I can't see her," he said.

"But she must be there," said Amy. "I heard her." She ran over and kneeled down beside him. Then she put her head through the hole in the floor and peered around carefully.

At first, she feared the builder was right. But as her eyes adjusted to the shadowy darkness, she spotted a huddled heap of cream fur too far away to reach.

She quickly showed the builder what she'd discovered, and he took up another floorboard in the right place. Then Amy reached down into the gap and lifted out the bedraggled Siamese cat.

Willow snuggled into her arms and looked around at the assembled clan. "Thank you," she mewed very quietly. "I thought I was going to be there forever."

Everyone waited anxiously while the vet checked Willow's health. Then he smiled and said, "She'll be fine once she's had something to eat and drink."

"Sardines!" said Miss Pickle. "That's what she's going to have."

"I'd like some of those," said Bun.

"But they're not a good reason to get stuck under a floor," warned Isambard.

Miss Pickle beamed at Amy. "I can't thank you enough, my dear. How did you realize she was here?"

Amy hesitated. She couldn't tell her what really happened without revealing the secret of the necklace. "The idea just sort of came to me," she said eventually. "But it was Hilton who actually found her."

"Of course it was," said Miss Pickle. She bent down and patted the terrier's head. "And I'm going to get you the biggest, best bone you've ever had. You deserve it for finding my vanishing cat."

The End

Amy Wild, Animal Talker

Collect all of Amy's fun and fur-filled adventures!

The Secret Necklace

Amy is thrilled to discover she can talk to animals!
But making friends is harder than she thought...

The Musical Mouse

There's a singing mouse at Amy's school! Can Amy
find it a new home before the principal catches it?

The Mystery Cat

Amy has to track down the owners of a playful
orange cat who's lost his home...and his memory.

The Furry Detectives

Things have been going missing on the Island and
Amy suspects there's a thief at work.

The Great Sheep Race

Will Amy train the Island's sheep in time for her
school fair's big fundraiser – a Great Sheep Race?

The Star-Struck Parrot

Amy gets to be an extra in a movie shot on the
Island...but can she land Plato the parrot a part too?

The Lost Treasure

An ancient ring is discovered on the Island, sparking a
hunt for buried treasure...and causing chaos.

The Vanishing Cat

When one of the animals in the clan goes missing,
Amy faces her biggest mystery yet...